P9-EDP-082

...y School
...ast 1935 North
Cedar City, Utah 84720

SOLDIER GIRL

Soldier Girl

Richard A. Boning

Illustrated by

Joseph Forte

The Incredible Series

Barnell Loft, Ltd. Baldwin, New York

Copyright © 1975 by Dexter & Westbrook, Ltd.

All rights reserved. No part of this book may be reproduced in any form or by any electronic or mechanical means including information storage and retrieval systems without permission in writing from the publisher, except by a reviewer who may quote brief passages in a review. Library of Congress Catalog Number: 75-25470

Printed in the United States of America

International Standard Book Number: 0-87966-110-0

To

Mary-Eliza Wilson

It was a peaceful scene that morning of October 22, 1692. Autumn sunshine poured down while workers gathered up the harvest of pumpkins. Madeleine de Vercheres watched with pleasure. It was hard to believe there had ever been any trouble with the Iroquois. None had been seen in months. The alarm had been lifted at Castle Dangerous. Then Madeleine noticed something move at the edge of the forest. Instantly she froze.

7

Anxiously she tried to peer into the dark woods. Everything seemed peaceful. Yesterday her parents had been called to Montreal. She hated this wild land at the junction of the St. Lawrence and Richelieu Rivers. In two weeks she would sail for Paris. She could hardly wait. There she would be safe at the convent school. Suddenly something stirred among the trees.

"Don't turn around," Madeleine told Laviolette, who stood beside her. "Keep talking. As we walk, look across the clearing. Do you see anything in the forest?"

The eyes of the giant soldier widened in surprise. Then they twinkled as he gazed fondly at the fourteen-year-old girl. "Ah, Mam'selle Madeleine, always a little joke." A flock of blackbirds flew up from the edge of the forest. Before Madeleine could call out a warning, the clearing was filled with whooping Iroquois. In an instant the peaceful harvest scene became one of horror. The French settlers raced towards the fort as painted warriors pursued them. Tomahawks flashed.

The next thing she knew, Laviolette had streaked into
the middle of a ring of warriors. Swinging his musket, he
bowled over half a dozen Iroquois. "Run, Mam'selle!"
he yelled. "Run!" Slowly his great strength gave way and
he disappeared under a swarm of Indians.

Now Madeleine stood rooted in terror as she watched old François, the cripple, hobbling along a row of pumpkins. Behind him bounded an Iroquois brave. Pitifully the old man turned to protect himself with his sickle. Before he could raise it, an ax glittered — and François crumpled.

11

Then a brave caught sight of Madeleine. He pointed at her with a shriek of delight. A group of Indians raced toward her, yelling madly. Madeleine turned and fled. The sound of feet grew closer. As the Iroquois narrowed the gap, their yells became triumphant. Even if she reached the fort, what could she do? Inside there were only two soldiers, half a dozen women, her two young brothers, and an eighty-year-old man. Just when it seemed that the Iroquois must overtake her, she was through the entrance. The gate slammed shut behind her. Swiftly the gate was barred.

"Where are the soldiers?" gasped Madeleine.

"They're in the blockhouse," Katherine, the cook, told her. Nimbly Madeleine raced up the ladder to the soldiers. They would help!

Then she saw a sight that filled her with horror. One soldier was holding a torch over a barrel of gunpowder, his eyes crazed with fear. The other stood there trembling, his fingers in his ears and his eyes closed.

"What are you doing?" Madeleine shrieked, appalled.

"Better to kill ourselves," said the one called Gahlet, "than to fall into the hands of the Iroquois." He moved to drop the torch into the barrel.

Madeleine's terror turned to fury. She was enraged that these soldiers would kill themselves rather than fight. "You miserable cowards!" she yelled.

Through the loophole she could see the field swarming with Iroquois — at least fifty of them. Seizing the torch, she touched it to the cannon. As it roared, the floor seemed to sway beneath her feet. When the smoke cleared away, the field was empty. But Madeleine knew that all she had done was to gain a little time. The Indians would be back all too soon.

Quickly Madeleine scrambled back down the ladder, her heart hammering wildly. At any moment the Iroquois would be swarming over the top of the stockade. Behind her came the two shamefaced soldiers. "To arms!" she shouted. "To arms!" Six women and her two young brothers, Louis, twelve, and Alexandre, ten, stared at her in disbelief. The eighty-year-old man hobbled up with his musket. Then a realization hit Madeleine with almost physical force. If they were to survive, everything would have to depend upon her alone.

She fought to steady herself. What could be done? Trying to speak calmly, she said, "Bring all the muskets from the blockhouse. Some will load. The rest will shoot. Move from loophole to loophole. Maybe they will believe we are fully manned."

Then Alexandre made a discovery that added to Madeleine's terror. "Look at the river!" he said in awe.

Madeleine looked at the St. Lawrence and gasped. In a small boat was Pierre Fontaine, a neighboring farmer. With him were his wife and two children. Now she knew why the Iroquois had become so quiet. As soon as the Fontaines set foot on shore, they would be slaughtered. Should she shout a warning? If she did, the Indians would open fire, and the Fontaines would die on the spot. Quickly she summoned the soldiers.

"Go down to the dock," she ordered. "Escort the Fontaines back here." But as she said it, the soldiers turned chalk white. Their eyes rolled in panic.

Then Madeleine realized that if the Fontaines were to be saved, there was only one person to do it. Overwhelmed, she groaned inwardly, but to her astonishment found herself saying, "Very well, I will go. Open the gates."

As Madeleine walked through the gates her heart hammered wildly. In moments her mouth was dry. She could feel the pitiless gaze of many warriors. Two hundred yards away Pierre Fontaine's boat was approaching the landing. Numbly she hoped the Iroquois would hold their fire. Perhaps they would be so surprised that they would wait to see what would happen next.

The Fontaines climbed out of the boat. Madeleine wanted desperately to run back to the fort. Somehow she found she was able to pretend that nothing was wrong. She managed to wave gaily, even though she expected to feel an arrow at any moment.

In what seemed hours she reached the landing. Still there was no sound from the woods. In a daze she welcomed the Fontaines.

"Mam'selle Madeleine," greeted Pierre. "We heard there were Indians on the river. We came to ask your hospitality for a few days."

Did she dare to tell them that death was only inches away? The Fontaines might panic and begin to run. That would be the end for all of them. She tried to smile, but she felt as if her face would crack. "You are more than welcome," she said. They strolled slowly toward the fort. They neared the gate. In just a few moments they would be inside. Madeleine felt dizzy from the strain. The walls seemed to waver before her eyes as if she were under water. Then they were through the gate.

"Close the gates," she told Gahlet. But he was motionless with fear. Quickly Madeleine closed them herself. Then she hastily explained the situation to the Fontaines. They listened with mounting terror.

"I will help," said Fontaine. "At least I can provide you with another defender."

"Another victim," said his wife in hushed tones.

22

Madeleine, still dazed from her experience, had no time to think of herself. A long war whoop rang out! It seemed to quiver with rage. The Iroquois had been outwitted, and they now sought revenge. As Madeleine looked through a loophole, the field suddenly seemed alive with warriors. Raising her musket, she remembered the countless hours of training her father, the Sieur de Vercheres, had given her. She had become a remarkable shot, but she had never fired at a living target. Then she recalled an expression her father often used. "Fire at will," she told the others.

Leading the charge was a huge brave. She could see a ring of bear teeth around his neck. Evidently he was an important warrior. Pointing her musket directly at his chest, Madeleine pulled the trigger. Through the smoke she could see him crumple, a look of astonishment on his face.

Again and again Katherine handed her a fresh musket. Again and again she fired. Now the enemy was only a few feet away. Then just at its crest, the attack wavered and broke. To her surprise the Iroquois were retreating. "They're leaving," Madeleine said to Katherine. "Let me have another musket." She turned and saw Katherine lying still on the ground. A musket ball had struck her in the chest. She was dead.

As Madeleine's brothers stood guard, Katherine was buried. After a simple prayer, Gahlet said, "She may be the luckiest of all." Everyone knew his meaning. A quick death was preferable to torture at the hands of the Iroquois.

"Maybe they will not come back," Louis said. But Madeleine knew better. The Iroquois were merely waiting for darkness. To make matters worse, she saw gray clouds in the distance. Soon it would snow. Under cover of the storm the Indians would overrun the fort at night.

But where would they attack? Often she had heard the Sieur say, "To fight the Iroquois you must think like the Iroquois." She had noticed a gully that led from the forest almost to the fort. The Indians had not used it in daylight, because they knew that gunfire would tear great holes in their ranks as they came out. But what about at night? They could reach the fort without being seen. The night would cover them.

Madeleine made an important decision. Taking a deep breath, she ordered, "Train the cannon on the opening of the gully."

The ancient weapon was aimed at the opening and locked into position. Under her direction her brothers had loaded the cannon with grapeshot, pieces of chain, bolts, nails, and broken glass.

As soon as it became dark, Alexandre crept out of the fort. At the opening of the gully he placed a number of stakes, connected by strips of leather. To the strips he attached all of the sleigh bells that could be found in the fort. Then quickly he slipped back inside.

Throughout the stormy night Madeleine listened closely. Hours went by. Had her plan failed? Were the Iroquois surrounding the fort even now? Then she heard a faint jingling noise.

"Fire!" she commanded. The cannon roared. A deadly hail whizzed into the gully. It was followed immediately by a chorus of shrieks, groans, and cries of pain. Once again the Iroquois had been stopped. Would they give up now? Dawn would tell the story.

Daylight brought a mystery that baffled and frightened her. The Iroquois were not leaving. Instead, their forces were growing much larger. Why all the warriors to take this one small fort?

Twice that day the Iroquois attacked. Each time they were driven back by the cannon. The grapeshot kept them from overrunning the fort. At night Madeleine beat on a drum. Periodically she called the hour and shouted, "All is well!" The other defenders also called from their posts. The fort sounded as if it were fully manned. That night there was no attack.

The days and nights began to blur together. Madeleine became dizzy from lack of sleep. She had lost track of time. Between battles the others slept, but somehow she remained awake. At times her mind would wander. . . . As a little girl she had listened to her father tell her about Paris. She could see the convent school he had described. She could hear the vesper bells ringing. It felt so good to be safe and away from the violence of New France. . . . Then she would arouse herself, only to find that she was still at the fort. Always she was aware of the growing number of enemy canoes.

On the afternoon of the seventh day, Madeleine was to
learn the answer. "Look!" blurted Louis. The edge of the
clearing was lined with braves.

"Mon Dieu!" said Louis in a choked voice. "So many! Why so many?"

Suddenly a chief stepped before the group of Indians. He spoke contemptuously, "Men of the Iroquois, six suns have passed, still you have not crushed this tiny fort. If you cannot crush this fort, how can you take Montreal? Up and down the river your brothers await news of our victory. As soon as they hear, they will join us."

Now at last Madeleine knew the answer to the mystery. Castle Dangerous lay in the path of an attack on Montreal. The small fort was doomed.

Turning, the chief faced the small fort. "Sing your death song, white men," he chanted. "The women of the Long House now build fires to roast you."

"Ey-ya, ey-ya," the braves chanted.

At these words Madeleine felt her blood run cold. Disdainfully the chief strode toward the fort to show his lack of fear. But Madeleine noticed that he was still out of musket range. As she watched in horror, the chief spread sticks on the ground. Warriors picked them up. As they did, they received a wooden shield and a torch. These were the bravest — *The Men of the Sticks* — the first wave of an attack. There would be no retreat. *Men of the Sticks* would fight to the death. Smoke from the torches rose to the top of the clearing. Madeleine's ears rang with the shrill cries. Even grapeshot could not help now. Then she had an idea. There was still one last desperate chance.

"Run," she told Louis. "Run and bring the telescope."

Scornfully the chief chanted, "A gun of magic that sees at night — soldiers who never sleep. Oh, *Ongue Honwe,* unbeatable men, do not be deceived. Now your eyes will tell you who has the greater magic." He raised his arms. Exposing his chest, he called out to the fort. "White soldiers, let us see your gun of magic."

Madeleine loaded her musket with a heavy charge. Taking the telescope from Louis, she lashed it to the top of the musket with a piece of cloth from her skirt. Now she must see if she could find the range. She decided to test the gun on a pumpkin. Sighting the musket through the telescope, Madeleine squeezed the trigger. Dirt spurted up three paces in front of the pumpkin.

The voice of the chief rang with mockery. To his warriors he chanted, "Oh, men of the Long House, their
magic is powerless before mine."

"Ey-ya, ey-ya," the braves replied.

Madeleine knew she must hurry. Loading again, she
sighted through the telescope, aiming a little higher. She
fired, and the pumpkin seemed to explode.

Now the braves were in a frenzy. As the leader raised his arm to signal the attack, all began pressing forward. In a moment they would sweep across the field.

Madeleine trained the telescope directly on the chief. It was a longer shot than any she had ever made. She fired. For a moment she could not see through the heavy smoke from the large charge of powder. Had she missed? Then she saw the chief, motionless on the ground.

A cry of rage went up from the Iroquois. Would they charge?

"Fire the cannon quickly!" shouted Madeleine. Louis touched it off. Grapeshot whistled through the autumn air. Braves crumpled. For a moment the warriors hesitated. Then the entire group disappeared into the forest carrying their dead with them. Once again the field was empty. Would they return?

For a long time Madeleine peered across the clearing. Now it was dusk. Perhaps the Iroquois had given up.

Then she could hear footsteps approaching. With a start she pulled herself together. The enemy was returning. Suddenly she felt no fear. Now when the end was near, she understood why her father had refused to leave his land. He had fought for it. She knew the same feeling. She would die fighting.

"Halt!" she warned, raising her musket. "Who goes there?"

To her amazement a voice answered in perfect French. "Lieutenant LaMonnerie."

When the Lieutenant and his men were admitted, LaMonnerie was astonished by the story he heard. But it fitted perfectly with what he knew. For some reason, every Iroquois along the river seemed to have vanished.

With great respect, he asked, "Mam'selle Madeleine, what can we do for you? You have saved Castle Dangerous — and Montreal."

She answered, "Relieve the others. They have been on duty for a week."

The soldiers quickly obeyed.

"But for *you*, Mam'selle, what can we do?" LaMonnerie asked again.

"Let me sleep," she begged.

Madeleine retired to her room. She had some news for the Sieur when he returned. She was going to stay in New France. In moments Madeleine de Vercheres enjoyed her first sleep in seven days.